Quarry

Célia Houdart

QUARRY

Translated from the French by K. E. Gormley

DALKEY ARCHIVE PRESS

McLean, IL / Dublin

Library of Congress Cataloging-in-Publication Data

Names: Houdart, Célia, author. | Gormley, K. E., translator.

Title: Quarry / Célia Houdart ; translated from the French by K.E. Gormley.

Other titles: Carrare. English

Description: First edition. McLean, IL : Dalkey Archive Press, 2020. Originally published by Éditions P.O.L. as Carrare in 2011. Translated into English from French.

Summary: "In Pisa, Italy, an Armenian immigrant named Marco Ipranossian sits in jail awaiting judgment on the attempted murder of a local official. The novel opens on the first day of his hearing-three years after his arrest-and follows the lives of (among others) Marco, his friends on the outside, the judge presiding over his case, her husband, and their teenage daughter, Lea. Though deceptively structured as a crime novel, Quarry's real concerns are both far smaller and far larger than those of a typical whodunit. Houdart's modern tale, presented in a series of brief, elliptical snapshots, is a precision-cut gem of literary minimalism"-- Provided by publisher.

Identifiers: LCCN 2019043660 | ISBN 9781628973273 (trade paperback ; acid-free paper)

Classification: LCC PQ2708.O873 C3713 2020 | DDC 843/.92--dc23

LC record available at https://lccn.loc.gov/2019043660

www.dalkeyarchive.com
McLean, IL / Dublin

Printed on permanent/durable acid-free paper.

Translator's Preface

THE FIRST TIME I read *Quarry*, I raced through it scanning for clues, intent on solving the mystery myself before the solution was handed to me at the end. When I reached the final page, I felt like I'd been tricked into running off a cliff. Where was the "big reveal"? What had I missed?

What I'd missed was, unfortunately, almost everything. *Quarry* is one of those odd works of fiction whose very genre—in this case, what the French call a *polar*, roughly equivalent to a thriller or crime novel—is a kind of MacGuffin. But, frustrated as I was, Houdart's clean, concise prose had made such an impression on me that I was willing to try again. And this time, I realized that what I really had in my hands was a manual on the hows and whys of reading, complete with a startling variety of object lessons both exemplary and cautionary. For instance, there's Marian in her office in 5, reviewing the official police report on the Marco Ipranossian case. She notices the document's irregular spacing, missing capitals, and mid-sentence carriage returns, but fails to "read" these signs correctly, though the information they contain is crucial, even central, to the nature of the case. An apt analogy, I think, for my own wrong-footed first run through the novel. Many chapters later, a character appears who would have been incapable of reading this report in the traditional sense, but who, I feel sure, would have been more sensitive than Marian to its typographical oddities, and might well have decoded them more readily than she did.

Nearly every character, in fact, grapples with issues of vision, reading, or textual interpretation. It is a testament to Houdart's skill that she can return to the same themes over and over again without ever seeming repetitive. Her writing is always natural, unobtrusive, effortless; never heavy-handed or forced. I've tried to preserve this light touch in my translation.

Another feature I've tried to reproduce is a sense of off-centeredness I can only call baroque, strange as the word might seem when applied to a pared-down, almost minimalist novel like this one. In Velázquez's baroque masterpiece *Las Meninas*, viewers are invited to use the vertical edge of the painting-within-a-painting as the visual boundary (effectively lopping a bit off the left side of the canvas), thereby reframing the scene and shifting its focus in a subtle but profound way. Because then it is no longer the young princess who occupies the center of the picture but a minor background figure, the man silhouetted in the brightly lit doorway of the far wall, who seems to have been caught in the act of either slipping in or slipping out of the room. Houdart effects a similarly subversive shift in her novel, away from the power players who are supposedly the center of the plot and onto the ordinary, often nameless characters who would normally be consigned to the background. But she reverses Velázquez's image: it is ironic, but perhaps not coincidental, that the victim of the assassination attempt which sets the plot of *Quarry* in motion is a man in a dim room standing silhouetted against the light, and that his assailant is the same. They are two of a kind, MacGuffins to the core. They sink into the novel like pebbles into a pond, without disturbing the smooth, calm surface that so beautifully catches the light.

Quarry

Célia Houdart

1

AT THE COUNTER of a café that had recently changed owners, Marian asked for an espresso and an apricot croissant. Blurred reflections slid over the brushed stainless steel: hands reaching out to greet newcomers, the constant shuffle of cups and water glasses.

Next, Marian headed to the north side of the city. The radial roads converging on the Piazza dei Cavalieri were filled with students. Skinny jeans. Hair plastered to the forehead or sculpted with gel in front of the mirror. Bicycles swerving to avoid couples with their arms wrapped around each other's waists.

The courthouse, which dated from the 1930s, had an imposing facade pierced vertically by three rectangular openings surmounted by a loggia. At the entrance stood two *carabinieri*, one a very young man. A court reporter on the stairway was digging inside the arm of his jacket, trying to straighten a twisted shirtsleeve.

Marian's office was small, with pale gray walls. She picked the dead blooms off a pink azalea and let them fall into the wastebasket in a rain of petals, thinking about what she'd have to say on this, the second day of the hearing. She took off her raincoat and slipped her robe on over her street clothes.

The courthouse lobby was already resounding with voices that could be heard echoing up the stairs. Marian slid some files into a black leather portfolio. Then she looked around the office for a ring, an aquamarine that had once belonged to her mother. She wore it on the little finger of her right hand and, because it fit loosely, had gotten into the habit of rotating it around her finger with her thumb. She searched between books, lifted file trays. Nothing. Without that ring, she thought, she would be stumbling over her words when it came time to speak.

2

A POLICE VAN pulled up and parked in front of the courthouse steps. A man in a bulletproof vest emerged from the back holding another man—fortyish, brown-haired, thin—by the arm. They both had to duck coming out of the van because of their height. Once out, both stopped for a moment, blinded by the sun. At the same time, the driver got out and slammed the door. He went over to the young *carabiniere* at the entrance and handed him a plastic sleeve containing a sheet of light-blue paper and a ballpoint pen. While the young man was initialing the document, the other *carabiniere* asked the thin man to hold out his manacled wrists. The *carabiniere* put his hands pincerlike over the steel cuffs and gently slid them forward. He checked the lock housings and the stress-bearing joints. The light glinting off the metal bothered him. He had to squint to see clearly. Then the two *carabinieri* positioned themselves on either side of the thin man and grabbed him by the arms. The older one gave a curt order in a faint Neapolitan accent and gestured at the stairs in front of them with his chin.

They entered a cavernous lobby striped with thin ribbons of sunlight. All three men wore rubber-soled shoes. They moved noiselessly. Their progress through the courthouse had a ghostly quality to it. The thin man was dressed in a black suit jacket missing several buttons, a white dress shirt, and charcoal-gray pants that were slightly too large.

In the hallway, some jurors were checking their summonses. They were familiar with the building but had been disoriented by new a signage system and wanted to make sure they hadn't wandered into the wrong wing.

Both double doors of the courtroom stood open. The *carabinieri* escorted the thin man to a chair on a low dais and made him sit. From here he had a view of the entire room. It seemed to him that there were far fewer people than there had been the day before. Against the wall to his right was a row of benches whose sagging leatherette formed a series of strange, melted craters.

3

THREE YEARS EARLIER, at the beginning of July, the
prefect of Pisa had been vacationing with his wife in a
rented villa on the island of Elba. It was the siesta hour.
His wife was reading by the pool. A big red beach towel
lay drying on the diving board. The prefect was in his
bedroom, stretched out on the bed, taking a nap. A man
entered the house through the living-room bay window,
which had been left open a crack. He emptied out a chest
of drawers, taking some designer scarves and an Olympus
camera. The sound of the lens cap falling onto the tile
floor woke the prefect. He sat bolt upright in bed. He
called out to his wife, but because the pool was at the
other end of the yard she didn't hear him. When the man
saw the prefect's silhouette against the light, he fired
three shots in his direction and then fled, scrambling
over the metal gate at the end of the driveway.

They were later able to reconstruct his path thanks
to a network of fine black hoses which had been torn
out of the lawn, revealing that the man had tripped over
the automatic sprinkler system in two specific locations.

The prefect, meanwhile, took a few staggering steps and then fell. He struck his temple on a doorjamb and lost consciousness, a nine-millimeter bullet lodged in his right lung. He spent five weeks in critical condition at the San Martino e Frediano Hospital. Short-term memory problems and breathing difficulties had plagued him ever since. The feeling of wool caught in his throat persisted to this day.

On August 1 of the same year, the police arrested Marco Ipranossian, an Armenian, at the Florence train station. In a small leatherette pouch tucked inside his shirt they found a forged car title and a dry-cleaning slip with the address of a trattoria in Rio nell'Elba written on the back.

4

THE ENTRANCE OF the jurors altered the acoustics of the room, dampening its sounds. A brunette woman—pale pink suit, pistachio blouse, hair in a bun—sat down in the front row. She took a little notebook and a miniature pencil from her beige leather bag. Sitting behind her was a tall man of about fifty in dark glasses. From time to time he removed them to dab at his conjunctivitis-reddened eyes with the corner of a handkerchief.

The hearing began with the prefect summarizing his testimony from the previous day. He said he thought the man who shot him had been stockier. But he couldn't be sure. When first questioned, he had described a man of average build seen only in outline, with the light behind him. Marco Ipranossian's lawyer, Mr. Onofrio, was scarcely twenty-five years old and had been assigned to his case by legal aid. He spoke very rapidly, sometimes giving the impression of not pausing for breath. On the first day of the hearing, Mr. Onofrio had moved that his client be released for lack of evidence. The motion had been denied. Today, as he was presenting his client's life story, the woman in the front row looked up from her notebook and studied Marco Ipranossian with interest. She saw little resemblance to the photo that had appeared in *Il Tirreno* the summer of his arrest. The man in the second row, whose conjunctivitis was reacting badly to the frigid air emitted by the malfunctioning air-conditioning system, listened to the proceedings with his eyes closed, mentally following the images conjured up by each speaker.

When the bells of the San Zeno Church struck noon, Marco Ipranossian was sitting hunched over in his seat. He was listening. He drew his cuffed hands closer to his chest, bent and unbent his numbed fingers to rid them of the pins and needles. He contemplated the hollow formed by the tendon between his thumb and wrist, into which, as a child, he used to pour sand or granulated sugar.

5

AFTER THE FIVE-AND-A-HALF-HOUR hearing, Marian sat alone in her office, leaning her elbows on the desk blotter. Faces and isolated details of the day came back to her: the prefect's nervous tics, Marco Ipranossian's composure, his green eyes, the worried look that crossed the face of his lawyer, Mr. Onofrio, every time he glanced at his client for support.

She slid a copy of the official case report from a large envelope. She read the first few lines. The words were irregularly spaced. There were typos, carriage returns in the middle of sentences, missing capitals. Had the clerk had trouble with the electric typewriter? Had he been distracted? Marian thought of her husband, Andrea, who in the course of his work might have to analyze— and puzzle over for hours—a single flaw in the weft of a fabric, a knot, a wax stain, which he would examine with a loupe, methodically analyzing the clues he found in each of them.

Sunlight now flooded the office. Marian took off her

judge's robe. She fished around in the bottom of the garment with one hand and threaded a hanger up inside the black lining.

The window was open. Every so often, the whine of a distant buzz saw or the twittering of swallows would filter in. There was a soft breeze. The robe, now hanging on a coatrack, oscillated gently from side to side on its little gold hook. Marian looked out at the city rooftops, the Leaning Tower, the rectangle of the Camposanto, and the clouds rolling in from the sea.

She poured herself a glass of club soda and continued reading.

*

Out in the police van, Marco Ipranossian was looking at the shadow under the chin of the *carabiniere* seated across from him, motionless and sweating in his bullet-proof vest. The window between the passengers' area and the cab was protected by a diamond-mesh metal grille caked with remnants of the dirt and small, dry leaves that were sometimes blown in when the rear door was opened, depending on the air currents.

6

ANDREA AND MARIAN first met in a university dining hall in Pisa when they were students. Andrea had been immediately attracted to Marian's lithe figure, her long, frizzy brown hair, and the way she had, on that particular day, turned around to look over her shoulder at a movie-club poster someone was pointing out to her. A few days later, they ran into each other again at a birthday party hosted by one Francesco Brusatin, a math major who was a mutual friend. They talked for a long time, sitting on a mattress and drinking fizzy, strawberry-scented local wine out of plastic cups. Later someone put on a dance record.

Marian had been born in Florence to an Italian father and an American mother who wanted to name her daughter after her grandmother in Massachusetts. When her parents divorced, Marian, then fourteen, stayed with her father. Her mother returned to the United States, to live in a little studio apartment in Oakland.

Marian was studying Roman law when she met

Andrea. He was finishing his PhD thesis on ancient South-Indian textiles. After earning his degree, Andrea got a postdoc fellowship in Berkeley's South & Southeast Asian Studies Department. Marian joined him six months later to take a course on the history of law and legal theory. They lived in California for two years. It was there that Lea, now fifteen, had been born. Marian's mother spent many hours babysitting her granddaughter while Marian and Andrea were at Berkeley. After that, Marian sat for the Italian National Judicial Council entrance exam and did a few internships in Rome. She, Andrea, and Lea spent eight months living in a garret studio apartment on Via dell'Oca. Then an examining magistrate position had opened up in Pisa.

Andrea, on the other hand, had still not managed to find a job in his field. Recently, some colleagues had suggested he apply to the University of Siena's Foreign Language Department, encouraging him to start a Hindi program there. Andrea put together a proposal and requested a meeting with the university president.

While he waited for a response, Andrea spent his days in their apartment on Via Turati, translating articles from the *Bulletin de l'Ecole française d'Extrême-Orient* into Italian, studying photomicrographs of ancient textiles sent by colleagues in Berkeley, and touching up the grout between the glass mosaic wall tiles in the bathroom.

7

LEA RACED DOWN the stairs. Out on Via Turati, a florist's black Lancia station wagon was parked in front of the Hotel Carducci. A deliveryman was lifting a bouquet of Casablanca lilies out of the back. The car's four-way flashers were reflected in the hotel's glass door. A little boy sat in the driver's seat, flipping through all the pre-set radio stations. He seemed to be a fan of heavy bass. Within seconds, the intense fragrance of the lilies had left an enticing, invisible wake in a sinuous path from the back of the Lancia to the hotel lobby.

Lea readjusted the wool bag she had slung over her shoulder. She held it in place with one hand and began to run. She felt the air on her face. Her navy-blue polyester shirt was flattened against her chest and arms. The sun was just starting to come up, gradually depriving the streetlights of their halos.

A street sweeper truck on Corso Italia was scrubbing the asphalt with its rotating bristles, leaving behind it a wide, dark ribbon that slowly faded from the edges inward. A man was darting from one side of the street to the other collecting cardboard boxes, which he folded flat and tucked under a bungee cord attached the back of the sweeper. Lea ran faster. She sprinted over the crosswalk that led to the train station, nearly out of breath. Her cheeks were bright red.

The train was filled with high-school students with their hoodies up and their hands buried deep in their pockets. Most were chatting among themselves. Two boys were sleeping, their Invicta backpacks propped against the window as makeshift pillows. A thin headphone cord squiggled a serpentine line down the front of a girl's shirt. All the students disembarked at Viareggio, some with their eyes still half shut, grumbling in protest.

At this point in the journey, Lea always tried to get a window seat on the right-hand side of the train. She wanted to watch the Apuan Alps rising in the distance, to read, at each station stop, the name written in white on the midnight-blue, enameled metal sign: first *Pietrasanta*, then *Forte dei Marmi*, *Montignoso*, and finally *Massa*—names that both daunted and fascinated her.

8

BECAUSE OF THE forged car title found on him the day of his arrest, Marco Ipranossian was initially suspected of being part of a criminal organization specializing in the alteration of stolen vehicles or the sale of phony paperwork. The subsequent investigation failed to turn up any evidence confirming either of these hypotheses. Nevertheless, the police did manage to piece together a few facts: Marco Ipranossian lived in a modest cinder-block house in a little town called San Jacopo, just north of Vicopisano. On Sunday afternoons and holidays, he frequently helped out at Primo Maggio, a restaurant in Buti. The rest of the time he used his considerable skill as a mechanic to repair cars on their way to the junkyard, cars he would later sell through classified ads.

According to the owner of Primo Maggio, who also owned the house in San Jacopo, Marco Ipranossian had few friends and had never been mixed up in any shady dealings.

*

The Buti restaurant was renowned for its antipasti and its dinner banquets. Vicopisano was also well known among local families. They often went there on weekends or public holidays to collect spring water from a fountain tucked away in a grove of hazel trees near the village entrance.

9

A WEEK AFTER the second hearing, the courthouse switchboard received an unusual call. A man was asking to speak to Marian about the Marco Ipranossian case. He was told it wasn't possible to put him through to a judge just like that. There was a procedure to be followed, a form he would have to pick up at the courthouse, and then a wait of at least three weeks before the judge would grant him an interview. The man answered in a mixture of standard Italian and dialect, of which at first the receptionist could understand nothing. He asked him to repeat himself. There was a pause. The receptionist heard rustling noises as the man put the phone against his chest. A second person, who must have been standing next to him, muttered a few words. The man came back on the line. Carefully enunciating each syllable, he talked about sheep, a dog, an impossible journey. The receptionist listened attentively. He asked the man for his phone number, promising he would call him back. More muffled whispers. Then the man, at someone's prompting, recited eight digits.

*

As the man replaced the cordless phone in its cradle, his companion saw the discouragement in his face. He picked up a nearby chair by its back and brought it closer.

"Here, sit," he said.

He smoothed out a tiny crease in the tablecloth. To make his guest feel better, he added, "I'm going to fix you a little something."

*

The man dined that night on walnut gnocchi, thinly sliced veal seasoned with lemon, and a *macédoine* of fresh fruit. Afterward, he had a cup of coffee and an *amaro* served in a small, thick-bottomed glass.

This was the shepherd of Buti. He'd telephoned from Primo Maggio. It was the owner, deeply moved by the Ipranossian case, who had encouraged him to testify.

10

MARCO IPRANOSSIAN AND Filippo, his thirtyish Calabrian cellmate, were lying on their beds and craning their necks to watch a TV that had been mounted too high on the wall. Marco Ipranossian had a cold; his eyes were puffy and red.

The presenter was a blond man with bangs. He sat on a stool in front of an American-style kitchen counter, talking up a line of cardio equipment and some animated, light-up wall art depicting waterfalls and leaping dolphins.

Short film clips of these products were playing on a continuous loop inside separate rectangles at the top of the screen. The presenter was dressed as if he were going to a wedding, in a shiny beige suit and a steel wristwatch that glittered under the studio lights. By referring to his own TV monitor, he could point out each item by gesturing at the empty space provided for it over his head. A jingle with prerecorded voice-overs and canned applause punctuated the broadcast, during which he took the opportunity to straighten the knot of his tie.

Filippo stood up. He had a headache, he said. He put a hand on his forehead to check for a fever. He said it was his turn to be seen.

*

When they weren't watching TV, Marco Ipranossian and Filippo paced around the narrow outdoor exercise yard. Or went to the visiting room. The rest of the time, they slept, read, or played dominoes.

*

Marco Ipranossian had emigrated from Armenia at the age of twenty-one. His mother had died of a red blood cell disorder when he was eight. She was originally from Prato, Italy. Marco Ipranossian had always promised himself he would visit the Tuscan city one day.

He quit school at fifteen and got a job at a mechanical-parts assembly plant north of Yerevan. He saved up a little money. He acquired the rudiments of Italian by memorizing sentences copied out of his mother's old books.

In June of 1984, he took an overnight train to Tbilisi. He went on to spend two days in Moscow. Then he took another train to Budapest, Munich, Milan, and Florence.

In Prato, the two female cousins of his mother's who still lived in the area gave him a very cool, almost hostile reception when he spoke to them over the phone.

Marco Ipranossian had spent one summer working at a gas station in Empoli. He had been just about to set off again when he had come across a help wanted ad placed by the owner of Primo Maggio.

11

AT THE CARRARA train station, flatcars laden with huge blocks of marble and granite crowded the marshaling yard. More blocks waited on pallets at the end of the loading platform. What had struck Lea on her first visit here was the enormous variety of stones in transit and the forest of loading cranes. The station was surrounded by processing plants and import–export companies, all of which had seen their business drop off sharply after the first oil crisis and the collapse of the Saudi market.

Lea's journey wasn't over when she reached the station. She still had a long bus ride ahead of her, down an avenue bordered by plane trees, tool shops, and foundries. She got off at the final stop, a town square with very black asphalt that looked like a parking lot. On the right was a persimmon tree, growing behind a chain-link fence in someone's garden.

As she always did on studio days, Lea stopped first at a corner store to buy a slice of focaccia wrapped in paper that soaked up its oil like a blotter. She ate her breakfast while walking to her next stop, L'Azzurro, a bar where a server with bushy eyebrows and rosacea-blotched cheeks mixed her a cup of thick Italian cocoa in a stainless-steel pot, tilting it at an angle to better release the steam. At nine o'clock, she saw the old man who always sat at the same table reading his newspaper and drinking barley coffee.

After that, Lea made her way to the Piazza XXVII Aprile, where the Valli Studio was. She passed a *salumeria* displaying in its window a slab of pork fatback coated with a mixture of salt, ashes, and aromatic herbs. On the same side of the street was a store selling hiking gear, the offices and library of the International Anarchist Federation, and a house with a cracked, crumbling facade whose louvered shutters were all tightly closed, except for one second-floor window where the two shutter panels seemed ready to burst open under the pressure of a luxuriant creeper vine in a flower box.

There was a market every morning at the end of this street. Today, a woman had stacked porcini mushrooms with slimy brown caps into neat pyramids on a red-and-white checked oilcloth. She was waving her hand over them to shoo away tiny flies while chatting with her neighbor, a middle-aged woman in a mauve knit shawl who was busy filling clear plastic tubs with green olives, capers, and pickled lupini beans.

12

ANDREA STEPPED OUT of the shower and wiped the fog from the bathroom mirror. He saw his face and salt-and-pepper hair emerge in the large *S* left by his palm.

Andrea wore his hair in a crew cut that he maintained himself. Today he set the blade of his electric clipper to three: a bit shorter than last week. His hairline had receded into two semi-circles meeting in a widow's peak, like an arrow pointing toward the slender bridge of his nose.

He pulled on a pair of jeans, a white shirt, and a red-and-green jacquard sweater. He sat down at his desk. Taped to the lower edge of his Power Macintosh's screen was a photo of a scrap of indigo fabric currently being preserved like a sacred relic at the Textile Museum in Washington, DC.

Among that morning's mail, Andrea found an envelope from the University of Siena. They were offering him an appointment in fifteen days' time. Had his application been successful?

He reached for a mug of strong black tea and brought it to his lips, telling himself as he sipped that it would help keep him from building castles in the air.

13

RUBBER HOSES HUNG down into the studio, connected by cross fittings to a metal compressor pipe that ran the length of the room. The pipe, in turn, was supported by a network of strings looped over the ceiling beams. The whole fragile apparatus shuddered with every blast of compressed air.

Seung Mi, a Korean student from the School of Fine Arts, was working a block of pink Portuguese marble. She was bent over the stone in her orange parka and ear protectors, her hair covered with a kerchief. A spot of color moved into her peripheral vision. She looked up and saw Lea across the room. She waved. Lea said hello in return, raising her voice in order to be heard over the din of the machines.

The studio workshops occupied the outbuildings of a former manor house—a mansion complete with double staircase, perron, and peristyle—of which the ninety-three-year-old signora Valli was the owner and sole occupant.

The entrance to the workshops was through a large pair of arched double doors covered by sheets of polyurethane. On rainy and windy days, workmen would anchor the sheets with two-by-fours.

Everything inside—the pneumatic hoses and hose stands, the tools and tripods, the clay models and the artists' faces—was white and coated with powder. When asked to describe the studio, Lea would say it made her think of a bakery, a plaster works, and the surface of the moon.

14

ONE MONTH AFTER the shepherd's phone call, Marian herself called the owner of Primo Maggio. She asked him to relay a message for her.

It was going on 5:00 p.m. The owner, an imposing man with large hands, gray eyes, and thick black eyebrows, wrote the words Marian dictated onto a leaf of the outdated agenda book he used as a scratch pad. Then he hung up and carefully tore out the page. He called to his son. A boy of eleven, wearing Bermuda shorts and a red fleece jacket, appeared in the doorway. He was in the middle of swallowing something. There was flour on his jacket. While no one was looking, he had been picking at the fresh gnocchi laid out on a table in the kitchen. His father read the note out loud to him. When he was finished, the boy took the paper, folded it, and left without a word.

The boy jumped on his bicycle and started off down the gravel-strewn Buti road. As he pedaled, he held a fine chain and its little silver medal in his mouth.

After passing the last of the houses, he dismounted and hid the bicycle in a ditch. Then he climbed a small hill. At the top of the hill was the shepherd, sitting on a pile of stones and bundled up like someone with the flu. The shepherd's dog recognized the boy. The boy and the shepherd saw each other from time to time. They had fished for crayfish together with little barbed forks. And the boy would occasionally watch over the sheep for pocket money.

The boy took out the piece of paper and unfolded it. He read it aloud to the shepherd. With the tips of two fingers, the shepherd pulled down the scarf that was covering his mouth, revealing a reddish beard. He thanked the boy. The dog circled around and around them, brushing against the child's bare legs. There was a tiny scrape above the boy's right knee.

*

That same day, Marian got word from the owner of Primo Maggio that a meeting had been arranged with the shepherd; it was to be one week later, in Vicopisano.

15

FILIPPO WAS SLEEPING in an unusual position: seated on the floor, legs stretched out in front of him, knees slightly bent, with one elbow propped on the edge of the bed and his cheek resting on the back of his hand. His mouth was open and he had a washcloth pressed to his forehead. Marco Ipranossian was sleeping, too. He was lying on his stomach holding a pillow over his head with both arms. His feet and part of his legs were sticking out from under the edge of the blanket. The gap between the men's beds was exactly 190 centimeters, wide enough to accommodate a small laminated table, which they usually pushed against the wall at night. Yellow-orange light from the tall sodium lamps in the courtyard filtered in through the window.

Suddenly, Marco Ipranossian, with one of those abrupt jolts that sometimes happen in dreams, woke with a jerk and pushed his head and chest off the mattress. He was staring straight ahead as if hypnotized. His pupils were dilated. He was sweating. He could feel his pulse pounding in his right temple. He stayed like this for a long moment. Then he relaxed his elbows and gently lowered himself back onto the bed. His breathing steadied. The terry-cloth mattress cover dried some of the sweat from his skin. His eyes lost their glassy stare and he looked around him. He noticed how the light fused the room into a single piece by washing everything in a uniform bath of color. His panic was slowly subsiding, when a noise broke the silence.

Marco Ipranossian understood then what had woken him. Filippo, in his sleep, was nudging an iron box of dominoes with his toe. The box scraping over the concrete floor made a series of high-pitched, staccato sounds, like Morse code.

16

THE PUBLIC SQUARE that served as the bus terminus
shimmered with puddles in which tiny twigs and dead
leaves lay steeping. It was mid-November. The dark
branches of the persimmon tree were bent under the
weight of their orange fruit.

Seung Mi, the Korean student, was almost finished
polishing her work in pink Portuguese marble. She
had transformed a long inclined plane into an abstract,
softly undulating bas-relief whose rhythms and contours
recalled eddies on the surface of a river.

The sculpture on which Lea had been working twice
a week was of white marble, a local variety veined with
light gray and a pale, creamy yellow. Lea had patiently
coaxed a form out of the raw block. She preferred to
work the marble by hand with a hammer and chisel,
willingly forgoing pneumatic power tools.

In middle school, during a field trip to the
Contemporary Arts Center in Prato organized by her
young art teacher, Mimmo, Lea had seen a colossal

Henry Moore sculpture that had made a profound impression on her. She had known then and there that she wanted to sculpt, and that what most appealed to her, even more than clay modeling, was a technique called *direct carving*.

The very next day, she had spoken about it to Mimmo, with whom she also took an art class on Tuesday evenings. This class met on the stage of a disused theater at number 38, Lungarno Antonio Pacinotti. It was a run-down building of faded opulence—ocher and brown walls, stuccoes, figures of lyres and curled acanthus leaves. Any paper or soft erasers the students left out overnight would be eaten by mice.

Mimmo had promptly recommended the Valli Studio in Carrara. She enrolled there a year later, after having been admitted to a part-time program at Galileo Galilei High School. Her parents agreed to the arrangement. Lea had a real gift for drawing and sculpture.

*

Lea straightened up. She considered the most recent modifications she had made. Then she bent down again and continued working.

Her plastic safety goggles emphasized the roundness of her forehead. Muscles could be seen tensing in her arms and jawline.

Out in the courtyard was a saw that ran day and night, cutting blocks of marble streaming with water.

17

THE LITTLE ROOM being used as a vestibule smelled of toner, floor wax, and printer paper. Andrea had been waiting here for over an hour, sitting in a molded plastic chair opposite the photocopier. An icy draft whistled at the keyholes and seeped in through the visible gaps under the doors. Andrea was freezing in his parka.

Professor Eduardo Foa, the university president, entered the room. He recognized Andrea at once. The two had crossed paths years ago in Rome at the home of a mutual friend, a bookseller who was also the founder of *L'occhio critico*, a cinema review whose editors met once a month at his apartment on Via del Parione.

The professor offered to take Andrea's parka, which he hung on a coatrack. He was a man of about sixty. Jovial. Magnetic stare. Silver hair swept back in a mane. Tweed jacket. Burgundy tie. A midnight-blue ribbon was sewn into his buttonhole. His powerful hands and arms were subject to strange, intermittent tremors, much as certain musicians, when gripped by a piece of music audible only to themselves, will go through the motions of play-ing it, will seem to *experience* it, physically. Andrea knew these tremors were simply one of the professor's quirks, not a sign of restlessness or neurological trouble.

Eduardo Foa's office occupied a spacious room on the second floor of the Palazzo Trecerchi-Piccolomini, complete with chevron parquet floors, coffered ceiling, and three deep-silled windows. An imposing bookcase in dark wood ran the length of the back wall. Two lapis-blue velvet armchairs had been set facing each other by of the windows for their interview.

The professor, with age, had become sensitive to the cold. At his request, the heat in his office had been turned up as high as it would go. Andrea ran through his résumé perched on the edge of his chair, feeling some-what ill at ease. His face was reddened as much by the drastic temperature change as by his nervousness.

The professor listened, chin in hand, brow furrowed, left eyebrow slightly raised.

He told Andrea about his long-standing ambition to create an institute of Eastern languages at Siena, while at the same time deploring the university's current state of affairs, which was hardly favorable to such initiatives. He was quick to point out, however, that he hadn't yet given up hope, and that if the project ever came to fruition, he would give Andrea a leading role in the Eastern Art History Department, as well as a post teaching Hindi. The professor wore a funny little smile on his face as he said all this.

On his way out the door, Andrea's eyes were drawn

to a painting he had scarcely noticed on coming in. The professor stepped aside to give him a better view.

It was a wood panel from the late sixteenth century, depicting Siena as a utopian city. Geometrical. Pink and blue. With Greek temples transplanted into the center of town, and terraces and palaces of composite styles, all lit by a radiant golden twilight.

In the lower right corner of the picture was a long-faced man in three-quarter profile. He was standing next to a dapple-gray horse and holding its vermilion bridle lightly in one hand.

18

Signora Valli liked to spend her Saturday mornings wandering through the vacant studio. She walked very slowly. She looked at the sculptures, their progressive stages of polishing, the little piles of sharp marble chips around newly begun pieces. High shelves around the studio were stocked with copies after the antique, generally scale models, whose naivete and clumsiness (toothpick arms, bulbous joints, gross asymmetries) endowed them with a bizarre sort of beauty.

On this particular visit, signora Valli was surprised to find a plaster hand standing upright on a workbench—a hand whose palm and finger pads had been pricked with the point of a compass. A fine circle had been drawn around each puncture mark in red pencil, as if to illustrate a lesson on Chinese medicine. On a tripod next to the hand was its replica in stone, still in the early stages. Signora Valli thought of her grandfather, a hero of the Tuscan Risorgimento who had suffered terrible powder burns on his fingers while loading a weapon. She could picture him clearly: a tall, gaunt, elderly man, forever trying to hide his hand at family gatherings by keeping it inside his coat pocket, or encased in a glove. That phantom hand had been an enduring object of curiosity for her as a child (it was only much later that she had been told of the injury) and it was no less a mystery to her now, as a grown woman.

Signora Valli resumed her silent walk through the aisles. Everywhere else, she was in constant fear of falling, but here in the studio she was perfectly at ease. The floor was somehow softer than other floors, more pleasant underfoot.

At noon, she ate lunch in her kitchen: *pasta al brodo*, to which she would add peas when they were in season, but which today she garnished with an egg. Then she sliced into the top of an orange with a paring knife. She cut away the peel in one long spiral, which she let fall gently into a shallow dish. She slept for an hour or so. Then she read through her mail, which a neighbor had left out on a piano bench for her.

She spent the rest of the day sitting in an armchair, sometimes dozing, sometimes awake. Watching the purple clusters of bougainvillea on the pergola outside the window as they stirred in the breeze.

It was going on six o'clock, and signora Valli felt a cold draft. She wrapped herself in a mohair blanket. She was a garnet figure against the faded blue wood paneling.

19

FILIPPO HAD HIS arms extended behind his back, fingers interlaced. He spoke to Marco Ipranossian as he stretched:

"You were talking in your sleep last night."

"It couldn't've been the guards out in the hall?"

"Nope."

"Sure?"

He dropped his arms, then said:

"Your lips were moving."

Marco Ipranossian showed no reaction. The prospect of discovering a hidden side of himself made him a little uneasy.

"Remember what I said?"

"It was bits and pieces."

Filippo pushed a lock of hair out of his eyes.

"At one point, you said something about 'little wild berries.'"

Marco Ipranossian thought about this for a moment. He saw the words floating in front of him. But there was no meaning behind them. He was still half asleep. Then all at once the pieces fell into place, like in a game of concentration when you spend a long time turning over mismatched cards and then suddenly get several pairs in a row. He saw a steeply sloping road. A large rectangle of concrete. Bright red berries in a child's palm. There was a bitter, acrid taste in his mouth. He connected the three words to a childhood memory from Yerevan.

On Spandaryan Street, near the old reservoirs, there was a vacant lot between two houses. A little island of countryside in the middle of the city. All kinds of wild plants grew there. He and his brother used to spend long afternoons playing in that lot. One day, on a dare, they ate some berries that were a weird shade of red, not the usual gooseberry red. They had tasted terrible. He and his brother had spit them out right away and gone running for the garden hose by the garage, where they gulped down water and rinsed out their mouths as best they could. They were sure they had eaten poison.

Marco Ipranossian had thought about the vacant lot on Spandaryan Street often, but this was the first time he had remembered this particular episode.

Just then, a guard's voice called from behind the door. Filippo was wanted in the visiting room. Prisoners were always notified at the very last minute. And then they might be left to wait in the room for an hour or more.

Filippo was still shirtless. He scrambled to get dressed. Head and arms flailing inside his sweatshirt.

*

Filippo had glossy black hair and olive skin flecked with moles. There was a scar below his right ear. He said he had been slashed with a box cutter one night when he was eighteen, as he was leaving a club during a party that had gotten out of hand.

20

Marco Ipranossian regularly wrote postcards to his father, which the owner of Primo Maggio would drop in the mailbox in Vicopisano for him.

He described changing seasons. Thunderstorms. Clear spells. Frosts. A kingfisher diving into the water. Forests of hazel trees. The colors on songbirds' bellies. The morning sun shining through the windows of his workshop. A day the electricity was out. A sunrise. A dead hare. An invasion of butterflies. Rare car models he had worked on. A dance in Buti. New wall fixtures in the main dining room at Primo Maggio. Tortellini with white wine, butter, and pancetta. The roasted kid goat with herbs and polenta that he had served to a hundred people on Easter Sunday.

He also talked about the owner's son and the shepherd, with whom he had burned brush piles and hunted poisonous snakes.

He asked for the latest news about his brother, who managed a mirror factory. He asked for family photographs, which he pasted into a spiral notebook.

He thanked his father for the packages of books he sent him.

He said nothing about what had happened. He didn't want to cause worry. And he didn't know how to explain that he had spent the last three years waiting for a court decision.

21

ON A SATURDAY afternoon near the end of November, Marian was driving a charcoal-gray Fiat Croma slowly down the narrow road from Pontedera to Vicopisano. As she rounded a curve, she saw a man in a tracksuit walking on the shoulder, followed by two women who looked like sisters. All three were carrying canteens. From the way they watched her pass, and the way she saw them squinting to make out the province code on her license plate when she glanced back in the rearview mirror, Marian got the impression that they were very anxious to know who she might be.

She was feeling somewhat anxious herself as she leaned over the steering wheel, on the lookout for road signs. Just when she thought she was well and truly lost, a sign reading *San Jacopo* finally appeared.

Olive orchards flanked both sides of the road. Around the base of each tree, bright green nets had been spread over the freshly turned earth.

The shepherd had entrusted the care of his sheep to

the owner's son for the day. He stood in front of a house, a few meters from the front door, arms crossed, waiting. He was wearing a dark green twill jacket; his red hair and beard had been neatly combed. His chest rose and fell rapidly. He felt as apprehensive as he had two months ago when calling the courthouse.

He heard a noise coming from down the lane.

A dip in the road hid the house from Marian's view. The tires and shock absorbers were not coping well with the rocky terrain. Bits of gravel kept pinging against the hubcaps.

When the shepherd saw the Fiat, he uncrossed his arms and waved to Marian with one hand, indicating a place near a big holly tree where she could park.

Marian got out of the car, knotting a silk scarf with a black-and-turquoise geometric print around her neck.

The shepherd and Marian walked over to each other and shook hands.

The car's engine made soft ticking sounds as it cooled.

The shepherd turned and looked over his shoulder.

"Here we are," he said. "Marco Ipranossian's house."

22

ANDREA'S INTERVIEW WITH Eduardo Foa had left him very discouraged. He wore the same tense expression that his friend Francesco Brusatin had noticed one winter Sunday twenty years earlier, after they had gone for a walk on the Marina di Pisa beach. They were sitting on the bus. Marian was there, too, with her long, frizzy brown hair and her smoky voice. The setting sun lit Andrea with a slanting, golden light that brought out every line of his face. Then Francesco Brusatin, with his mouth in the wry twist that meant he was about to say something serious under cover of a joke, had said: You look like a worried bird.

Andrea remembered the tin-roofed fishing huts and the big lift nets along the bus route. He remembered the outskirts of the former seaside resort that had seen better days. The bus stop at the end of a long, lonely boulevard. The row of palm trees on the median strip. The shops with boards nailed in Xs over their doors.

On the beach, Francesco Brusatin had rolled up the

cuffs of his jeans to wade in after scraps of driftwood
and dead seaweed. The beach had smelled like brine and
motor oil. The wind had tangled their hair. When it had
started to rain, they took shelter in a little café with a
view of the ocean.

*

Francesco Brusatin had married his childhood sweet-
heart after running into her again, purely by chance, on
a train journey. They settled in Trieste, where Francesco
was caring for his mother. She had always identified a
little too closely with Hollywood stars of the 1950s, and
by then she was rapidly losing her grip on reality.

The last time Andrea saw Francesco Brusatin was
in Trieste, at a restaurant on the Piazza Venezia that
served fresh seafood year-round. They had a long talk
over prawns, probing under the carapaces with their
knife tips for the coral.

23

MARIAN'S BLUE EYES turned to gaze at the door with its judicial wax seals. The shepherd said he had been looking after the place in Marco Ipranossian's absence: sorting the mail, putting the contents of drawers and cupboards searched by the police back in order, sweeping the leaves off the patio. Every once in a while, he would air out the entire house—this after he had noticed saltpeter forming on the dining-room furniture.

As he spoke, the shepherd demonstrated on one of the front left windows how he would open them from the top for the airings. Marian moved closer. Inside, she could see a tiled floor, a china cabinet, a table with mismatched chairs, a pile of mail held down with a blue-tinged rock.

The shepherd had known Marco Ipranossian ever since the latter's arrival in Vicopisano in 1984. They discovered that they had both been born in March 1963. They were also approximately the same height and weight, so they sometimes traded articles of clothing.

When the shepherd related this last detail, he cleared his throat, embarrassed. He broke off his story there. Then, as if to put an end to the awkwardness, he offered to show Marian another building. They circled around to the back of the house and stopped at a wooden shed. The shepherd pushed open the door, which had no lock. This was Marco Ipranossian's workshop. Car windshields, tires, a radio set, grease-blackened rags. On one wall was a big sheet of plywood with nails hammered into it for hanging tools. They had been arranged according to size and each one outlined in permanent marker. Some postcards had been thumbtacked to a cupboard door.

The shepherd noticed that it was Marian who seemed a little embarrassed now. He invited her to take a walk with him down to the river. They left the shed, ducked under a clothesline, and crossed a meadow.

They arrived at an embankment overgrown with reeds and bulrushes. Come summer, it would be swarming with mosquitos, said the shepherd. The riverbank dropped off sharply a few feet in front of them. They could see tree branches that had been swept away by the current and long, thin grasses pressed flat under the moving water.

The shepherd thought this would be a better place to talk. He picked up again where he had left off.

He said that, if he hadn't spoken up before, if he'd waited all this time, it was only because he'd been scared. He explained that he and Marco Ipranossian would often meet up at the flea market in Pontedera, where they would buy clothes from a secondhand dealer who'd become a friend of theirs. Marian didn't understand where this story could be going. The dealer, continued the shepherd, was from the town of Grosseto, some hundred and forty kilometers away. He crisscrossed the entire region collecting old clothes: individual donations as well as unsold or remaindered merchandise from shops. One of his main suppliers lived on the island of Elba.

At this point, the shepherd began rubbing his jaw, as if there were something he wanted to say but didn't quite know how. He paused. Then, choosing his words carefully, conscious of the effect they were going to have, he said that this supplier owned a dry cleaner's in Rio nell'Elba. And any clothes that were unclaimed after a year, he would sell in bulk.

"What kinds of clothes?" Marian asked.

"Jeans. Blazers. Suits and dress shirts left over from vacationers. One time, there was even a suede jacket."

"Did Marco Ipranossian wear clothes from this dry cleaner's?"

"Yes."

"He never went to Elba?"

"No."

As he spoke, the shepherd fished around in his pocket. He brought out a crumpled ticket with some writing on it. Two staples were still fastened to the top edge.

"The clothes dealer liked to tell us good places to eat, and he'd write the addresses on the backs of the dry-cleaning tickets. But I had no interest in taking the ferry, and neither did Marco Ipranossian."

*

The boy from Primo Maggio could be seen in the form of a silhouette overlooking the road to San Jacopo. He was sitting in the sun near a low wall constructed of stones with odd hollows in them, licked by generations of sheep searching for salt crystals.

24

THE DAY WAS almost over. Lea packed her tools back into her woolen bag—a vacation souvenir from the Peloponnese. Night was falling fast. A workman on a stepladder was busy wrapping a large sheet of tracing paper around a fluorescent ceiling fixture whose light had been deemed too harsh. Lea was about to leave, hurrying so as not to miss the 5:50 p.m. bus. She knocked over a plastic water bottle someone had left on the floor. She set it upright again. The rivulet of spilled water was instantly absorbed by the thick layer of powder, which in that part of the studio resembled dirty snow.

It was usually around this time of day, on the walk to the bus stop with her mind blank from exhaustion, that the image came to her: that of a girl her own age she had met in art class, a girl who had captivated her at first sight. Blond. Petite. With wide, expressive eyes and skin that seemed to drink in the light. As soon as the girl walked into the theater on Lungarno Antonio Pacinotti, everything else disappeared.

Lea carried this phosphorescent image with her through Carrara, aboard the bus, onto the windy train platform, on the train, and out into the streets of Pisa.

25

THE SHEPHERD AND Marian left the riverbank. The wind
had picked up. The air was suddenly cold. Marian was
wearing a gray pantsuit; she turned up the notched col-
lar of her jacket as she explained to the shepherd that
the revelations he had just made would be decisive to
the case and that his testimony needed to be taken down
in writing. She made it clear, however, that even if he
was reluctant to testify publicly at the hearing, which
was entirely understandable, he would still need to meet
with her again in the presence of a court clerk.

For a few seconds, the shepherd said nothing. He
stared straight ahead, as if looking at something very far
away or deep inside his own mind.

He said he would think about it.

A few holly leaves had fallen onto the hood of the
Fiat Croma. Marian drove away at a crawl over the dirt
road. It was getting dark. The boy from Primo Maggio
was bringing in the sheep for the night. Marian, startled
by the sudden appearance of the flock coming straight

toward her, responded by turning on her high beams. The boy put his hand to his eyes and cursed in dialect. The sheep scattered. Marian could feel them bumping their thick coats against the sides of the car. She was paralyzed for a moment, hands clutching the wheel, amid the sounds of bleating, barking, and the clatter of little hooves on the stony ground.

Far off in the distance, a few small, blue clouds hung motionless in the sky. The sun was a red disk sinking into the earth.

26

ON THE DRIVE home from Vicopisano, Marian had trouble getting back onto Via Turati. She finally left her car in a parking garage behind the train station. The entire neighborhood, all the way up to the Arno River, had been closed to vehicles.

Earlier that day, there had been a peace demonstration protesting the American military presence in the area between Pisa and Livorno, along the Navicelli Canal. The protesters had put stickers on shop windows and handed out flyers detailing the Pentagon's buildings policy, the 125 bunkers where they had stored bombs later used in the Yugoslav Wars and construction kits for building airstrips in combat zones.

Ever since the Bilateral Infrastructure Agreement of 1951, the city of Pisa and the United States had enjoyed a "special relationship," as local officials—and everyone else who profited from the deal, from developers to business owners—were fond of calling it. Consequently, the police kept a close watch on the regional pacifist movement, whose leaders, so they said, had ties to ex-members of the far-left Lotta Continua.

Marian had learned of this base from her mother, who had once mentioned a neighbor of hers in Oakland whose son, a fighter pilot in the US Navy, had been transferred to Camp Darby, in Tuscany, after five years at Hazebrouck.

A bit surprised, Marian had asked a fellow judge at the Pisa courthouse what he knew about it. He had photocopied a two-page spread from the daily newspaper *Il manifesto* for her that was dedicated entirely to Camp Darby.

Marian saw a small crowd of people inside a pharmacy. A young man in a denim jacket and turtleneck was holding his head in his hands. There was blood spattered on his Superga tennis shoes. His nose was bleeding and his hair was stuck to his skin with sweat. A pharmacist with her hand on his shoulder was speaking to him gently. Outside, a woman with a Florentine accent informed Marian that the boy's mother was a cashier at the clothing store Upim. He had been shoved headfirst into a newsstand during a police charge. He told the pharmacist he saw streaks and colored dots swimming before his eyes. It sounded serious. Marian, alarmed, immediately thought of Lea. Had she been among the protesters? Had she been injured? Marian felt goose bumps prickling her skin through her clothes.

*

Lea was in her room, sketching a bust of the goddess Hygieia. She thought of her friend from Mimmo's art class. The eyes were similar—slightly prominent. Broad forehead. High cheekbones. Hair pulled back, forming very soft, supple lines.

*

Marian stayed up till midnight poring over the documents in Marco Ipranossian's case file. She couldn't sleep. Andrea made her an herbal tea. She tried watching a nature documentary, but was unable to focus on the images of anemones and seahorses. She eventually lay down on the couch with her eyes open.

Mr. Onofrio had telephoned earlier that evening, around eight. His client had reiterated to him, during a conference in the visiting room, that he had not been carrying any forged car title the day of his arrest. His work permit was valid. His papers had been in order for the past eight years. He had no idea how the title had gotten into that leatherette pouch and from there into his case file.

Marian looked over the page listing the time, date, place, and circumstances of the arrest. A muscle twitched in her left cheek.

*

One week later, the shepherd gave his deposition. The appointment had been set for 10:30 a.m. at Primo

Maggio. The owner provided refreshments. The clerk ate several helpings of a smoked cheese that reminded him of his childhood in Basilicata.

27

IN EARLY MARCH, a new police team was assigned to the case. Two investigations were now being carried out simultaneously. The prefect, working behind the scenes, ensured that the atmosphere remained fiercely competitive. It was he who was calling the shots.

There was yet another search of Marco Ipranossian's house, and a reexamination of the Elba villa. No one was interested in renting the place these days. The paint was flaking on the swimming pool. The bamboo windscreen around the barbecue area had collapsed and lay in a heap on the paved walkway between the patio and the pool. There were ants in the cupboards.

The new lead inspector went around to all the neighboring villas and buzzed their intercoms.

This part of the island was deserted at this time of year. Only one neighbor answered his intercom. A retiree. He said that on the day of the shooting he had seen a suspicious-looking man, clearly suffering from a stiff knee or ankle, walking down the street in such a way that his weight was unevenly distributed. Forty-five years of age, perhaps. Brown hair. He could not remember his features. Was this the man who had tripped over the sprinkler system?

The retired neighbor spoke Italian with a nearly imperceptible accent.

"Are you Swiss?" asked the inspector.

"No."

"German, then?"

"Luxembourger."

*

The inspector spent nearly two hours sitting in an armchair facing the bay window. Then he had photographs taken of the lawn, which had transformed itself over the past three years into a meadow where anise and knapweed flourished in the spring.

28

Horse-racing season opened shortly before Easter. Buti's *Palio* was a modest affair compared with those of Parma and Siena, but it was the first of the year, and so everyone wanted to attend.

By 8:00 a.m., the crowds were already out in force. All along the city's main thoroughfare, which was bordered on one side by a long retaining wall, families took their seats on the parapet and sat dangling their feet over the edge. Folding chairs, stools, and benches lined the sidewalks everywhere else. The owner of Primo Maggio had put out his cane chairs. It was a black-and-white crowd still dressed in its winter wardrobe. Old men sat with their hands on their knees. Women leaned over to chat with their friends. Younger men stood with their arms folded or with a child perched on their shoulders.

Andrea, Marian, and Lea were there, too, leaning on a guardrail in the middle of a row of teenagers.

Loudspeakers on the lampposts were blaring music that partially drowned out the sound of voices. The streetlights' power cables stretched in taut lines across the sky. There were a few wispy clouds to be seen, and the moon was visible, though by now it was mid-afternoon.

The village was unrecognizable, emptied of cars and with sand covering its streets.

Suddenly, a voice from the loudspeakers announced that the horses were off. All heads turned as one to look in the same direction. The crowd held its breath.

29

Signora Valli stood in the doorway. She was looking at her bougainvillea. Giuseppe, one of the studio workmen, waved to her from behind the wheel of a pickup truck. She came out onto the front steps.

"On taxi duty already? Work ended early today," she said, smiling.

Lea, Seung Mi, and a young apprentice were sitting beside Giuseppe in the cab.

"I promised the kids I'd show them the quarries," he said. "Now's the perfect time of year for a visit. In the summer you can't see a thing, too much glare."

"Let me guess . . . Colonnata?"

"That's the one. Care to join us?"

Signora Valli heaved a deep sigh that was more sung than breathed, accompanied by a gesture—head tilted down, eyes closed, one hand raised to the level of her forehead, palm up, fingers spread—that expressed at once her love for the place, the memories it held, and her regret at no longer having the strength to go there.

*

From high up the steep mountain road, the town below looked tiny and gray. The blue-and-white Apuan Alps stood out against the horizon. Marble debris, like drifts of snow, covered them from summit to mid-slope. It had taken twenty minutes of potholes and hairpin turns to reach this point. Heavy winter rains had carved deep ruts in the road.

The pickup arrived at an overlook serving as a make-shift parking lot. From there, the road continued up the mountain but was much narrower and its use was reserved for the quarry workers.

On their right was a long, narrow, flat-roofed cottage with whitewashed walls. The word BAR had been hand-painted in black on the front. The lower ends of the letters were curled like the feet of wrought-iron chairs. Next to BAR was the singular SOUVENIR, whose block letters ran across a steel shutter that hadn't been fully raised. In front of the cottage, almost in the road, was a spinning postcard rack holding an array of dusty, faded snapshots of the quarries. There was a table of marble knickknacks: Davids, Pietàs, and Dianas, each one in front of its own polystyrene box; a few chess-boards and trivets. Inside the shop a neon light flickered and buzzed, and Bruce Springsteen was playing on the radio. The music seemed to come from a sort of storage closet. There was no one in sight.

Giuseppe suggested they keep walking. The path up the mountain was lined with disabled cranes and rusty metal signs warning them of danger from falling rocks.

The weather was getting hotter. The apprentice said the view reminded him of a place in northern Mexico.

30

MARIAN ATE LUNCH at the counter of the café, whose owner she now knew. He was a curly-haired Lebanese man whose specialties included pita sandwiches—these filled with prosciutto and grilled eggplant—and custards flavored with orange-blossom water.

Marian thought back to the time when she and Andrea had lived in Rome. Lea had been only two years old then. They were still living like college students. Andrea divided his time between the university library and the community center where he was working as a volunteer. Lea's daycare was in the same building, which also had a multipurpose room where there were occasional concerts, yoga classes, and a theater workshop taught by a rather oddball actress, also Lebanese, who had honed her craft at the Living Theatre.

Marian went to the register to pay for her lunch. Large mirrors on either side repeated her reflection to infinity.

The day was pleasantly warm. Out in front of the

courthouse, birds were wheeling and turning spirals on
the updrafts.

As Marian entered the lobby, she saw one of her fellow judges exchanging business cards with a lawyer. She
was trying to think of the actress's name. She ought
to know it—she had taken lessons with her. The name
Ipranossian kept coming to mind instead. It formed an
impenetrable barrier between her and her memories.

*

At around six that evening, Marian received a visit from
the court clerk. He asked her if they could talk. His
voice was unsteady. He said he was ashamed of himself
for not having had the courage to speak up sooner. He
wanted her to know that, from the first day of the Marco
Ipranossian hearings, he had been pressured. Marian
asked him to be more specific. His face changed and
went pale. He seemed unwilling to continue. Marian
insisted. They were alone, she said. He could speak
freely. He was still hesitant. He said that, if he told her,
it might mean trouble for both of them.

*

From that day on, Andrea was afraid for Marian. Mr.
Onofrio's friends and family also started to worry.

31

LEA MADE SLOW windmills with her arms as she walked. After the morning's studio work and the truck ride over (she had spent a long portion of the trip clutching the grab handle above the passenger door), her wrist and shoulder were aching. The footpath led directly up to a pass that the road reached only after several switchbacks. Gravel crunched under their feet. It was a fine day. Lea was at the head of the line. Seung Mi and the young apprentice came next, deep in conversation. Giuseppe brought up the rear. The little group picked its way slowly over the loose scree.

Halfway up the slope was a giant block of marble shaped like an irregular prism. Smooth, blindingly white, as solitary and majestic as those boulders carried into high valleys by glaciers that have long since melted. One side of the block, facing downhill, was conspicuously rougher and more jagged than the others.

Lea reached the pass and found herself on a high plateau. On her right was a mountain that seemed ready to lift the sky onto its shoulders. Someone seeing it from this standpoint would never guess the extent to which its flanks had been hollowed out by miners.

Seung Mi and the young apprentice were hanging back. They wanted to photograph the block from different angles. Giuseppe overtook them and arrived, winded, at the pass. Droplets of sweat clung to his eyelashes. For the first time, Lea noticed the network of tiny red capillaries around his nose. He ran a hand through his hair and said:

"Let's wait for them to catch up. We're going over that way next."

32

ANDREA REALLY WANTED to know the name of the horseman whose portrait he had seen in Siena. He spoke to a friend of his who was an art historian at the University of Pisa. The friend was unfamiliar with the painting in question, and his research was further delayed by the closure of several rooms in the art history library, where, after a recent flood, books on the ground floor were being dried by hand with hair dryers.

Finally, a month later, he found out the identity of the man depicted in the lower right corner of the scene. It was one Giovanni Battista Guarini, a poet and diplomat from Ferrara who had entered the service of Alfonso II d'Este and later served the Dukes of Tuscany.

He had published several books of poetry, some madrigals, and an essay, *Trattato della politica libertà*. He was also the author of a pastoral tragicomedy, *Il pastor fido*, which would go on to inspire works by Handel and Jean-Philippe Rameau.

His daughter Anna was murdered by her own husband in 1598. Guarini never recovered from the loss.

Giovanni Battista Guarini was included in the painting because he had been its patron. The equestrian outfit was an allusion to his love of horses.

Andrea was moved by this story. He invited his art historian friend out for a walk the same day. They sat in the sun at an outdoor café. They ate ice cream topped with candied fruit and rum raisins out of silver ice-cream cups.

Then they strolled around town, talking about this and that. Andrea confessed that he had given up hope of finding a job teaching Hindi. He would have to think of something else. He might even go into a different field altogether. But he honestly couldn't imagine what else he might do.

On the Camposanto, two little girls were walking through the grass in roller skates, none too steadily, their arms held straight out in front of them—the gait of people whose skis have come off halfway down a black-diamond slope.

33

Lea and her companions were some hundred meters from an immense quarry dating back to the reign of Emperor Tiberius. Five major benches, or levels, could be clearly distinguished, each of which was subdivided into a number of horizontal strips corresponding to different extraction zones. The strips formed a graduated series of shelves with only minor variations in depth. They were like a child's crude drawing of a staircase carved into the mountainside. Some parts were stained with vertical blackish streaks from storm-water runoff. Other areas were of a gray so pale it was almost white. At the inner corner of one bench was a protruding spur of rock with a fracture pattern suggesting it had been blasted with explosives. A long rope ran down its face. Its crevices were filled with chips of marble.

One hundred meters below, the underground quarry began. Lea and Giuseppe went to the edge of the path to look down into the gaping pit. The others stood back, saying it gave them vertigo. It was difficult to gauge the depth of the excavations or maintain any sense of scale.

Halfway down, a terrace-like ledge sparkled in the sun. At the very bottom was a basin filled with milky, pale green water. On the far side of the pit, they could see a muddy area with footprints around the base of what looked like a crane tower made of metal tubing. This was the ladder the quarrymen used to get in and out of the pit. There was no other access. At the bottom of the quarry, another, thinner rope dipped into the water. It went under a stone lintel and disappeared into a rectangular tunnel that must have been one of the adits.

The quarry was a wilderness of planes and angles, each catching the light in a different way.

Above the awestruck little group was a vast stretch of sky, partly veiled by clouds lighter than air.

34

MR. ONOFRIO, MARCO Ipranossian's lawyer, after having filed two motions for his client's release a full month apart, was threatening to bring suit in the European Court of Human Rights for a violation of Article 5, paragraph 4. He claimed the Italian courts had failed to respond "speedily" to his client's requests. He was also questioning the legality of Marco Ipranossian's detention.

The shepherd's testimony rendered all this moot. The grand jury dismissed the case.

Marco Ipranossian was released on April 11, 2005 at 10:30 a.m.

Neither he nor Filippo got any sleep the night before.

They gave each other one last, long hug. Then they said their tearful goodbyes.

*

As time went on, both Mr. Onofrio and Marian became

increasingly convinced that the attack on the prefect had been someone settling a score. But no one wanted to hear this theory. Not their colleagues at the courthouse, not the press, and especially not city hall.

*

The owner of Primo Maggio closed the restaurant for the day. He was waiting for Marco Ipranossian outside the Don Bosco Correctional Facility with a plastic bag containing a clean change of clothes, neatly ironed and folded.

That night, his son cooked dinner—a crayfish platter. He excused himself from the table around ten.

The owner of Primo Maggio, the shepherd, and Marco Ipranossian stayed up late into the night, eating hazelnuts out of the shell and drinking grappa.

*

In his cell, Filippo was lying in bed but couldn't sleep. He ran his hand absently over the moles and other marks on his skin.

35

TEN DAYS LATER, the prefect met with Marian in her office. His wife and his lawyer were there, too. The atmosphere was tense. As he sat down, the prefect pinched the creases of his trousers just above the knees to avoid stretching out the fabric. It was one of his habits. Marian brought them up to speed on the latest developments in the investigation. The Grosseto police had arrested a man the week before who was implicated in several burglaries along the Tyrrhenian coast. When the police searched his house, they found a Piombino-to-Rio Marina ferry ticket between the sofa cushions. They also found a handgun hidden in a shoebox. But the ticket was from the autumn of 2004 and the gun was the wrong caliber.

For several seconds, no one spoke. Marian looked the prefect directly in the eye.

"Marco Ipranossian was a convenient scapegoat for the two Pisan police teams right from the start," she said. "His arrest made life easier for a lot of people, didn't it?"

The prefect put his fist in front of his mouth and emitted a peculiar, high-pitched sound. Since his accident, he always cleared his throat before speaking, but this time the action seemed motivated mostly by embarrassment.

"If I understand you correctly, then, we're back at square one?"

"Yes," said Marian. "You could put it that way."

The prefect's wife was holding her purse on her lap. She clutched its handles tightly without saying a word. The lawyer snapped shut the metal latch of his briefcase.

*

The entire Ipranossian case file was contained in one thin, faded yellow folder.

On the mahogany desk lit by a slant of sun, a hemisphere of crystal in the shape of a bottle-stopper was simultaneously decomposing and recomposing the notes for an upcoming hearing.

36

THE SHEPHERD RAPPED on one of the shutters. It was his way of knocking. He had some books he wanted to return. Marco Ipranossian was in the bathroom, washing his face in warm water and rubbing the area between his cheekbones and hairline. He stopped still when he heard the tapping on the shutter, with his elbows pointed at the mirror and hands on his forehead. At that moment, he caught a glimpse of his mother's face in his own features: her eyebrows, which she used to redraw with a contour pencil, and her large eyes.

The shepherd was insistent. Marco Ipranossian draped a hand towel around his neck and hurried to the door.

Marco Ipranossian put on a pot of coffee.

He told the shepherd the books had been handed down to him from his grandfather, who was originally from Ashtarak, north of Yerevan. They were accounts of travels through the Orient, illustrated with engravings. Headdresses, ceremonial costumes, full-page pictures of architecture, scenes of rural life.

The shepherd loved beautiful books. Their language was always foreign to him, because he was unable to read. He turned the pages carefully. He studied the typefaces and the illustrations. These strange readings left a deep impression in his memory.

The shepherd picked up a book with a worn-out binding. He opened it to a page he had marked with a scrap of paper. He showed Marco Ipranossian the picture: a shepherd carrying a sheep across a river.

Marco Ipranossian looked at the picture, his black eyelashes motionless. He was transfixed. This was one of the first books his grandfather had shown him. He must have been five years old. An age when he couldn't read, either.

He asked the shepherd if he wanted milk in his coffee. "*Un'ombra.*"

*

The shepherd wanted to know all about the three years Marco Ipranossian had spent in jail. They weren't in the visiting room any longer. They didn't need to talk under their breath.

Marco Ipranossian described his friendship with Filippo. Their games of dominos. After talking for a while, his eyes welled with tears.

37

IT WAS THE season for cosmoses. The meadow sloping down to the riverbank was carpeted with them. The shepherd and the boy had sown them in March, the day after they found out Marco Ipranossian was going to be released. The shepherd always saved plant seeds from one year to the next. He kept them in elastic-banded envelopes laid flat in a drawer.

One morning, Marco Ipranossian went to Pisa in order to send something to Marian. The shepherd and the owner of Primo Maggio had told him all she had done for him. He had also made an appointment with Mr. Onofrio that afternoon. He wanted to give him a bottle of Armenian liquor he had found in an Asian grocery in Prato.

Marco Ipranossian went around the city on foot. The weather was beautiful. The sunlight lit his face.

Mr. Onofrio and another lawyer shared an office on the ground floor of a building on Via Oberdan. Marco Ipranossian rang the buzzer. Mr. Onofrio opened the door for him. With his checked shirt and his new growth of beard, he looked like a college student.

The young lawyer was touched by the gift. He asked Marco Ipranossian about his plans. He told him how pleased he was at the outcome of the case.

The two men shook hands.

As Mr. Onofrio watched Marco Ipranossian walk away, he felt sure he would never forget either the tone of his former client's voice or the look in his eyes.

*

Marco Ipranossian had planned to return home by the five o'clock train. He walked under the shelter of the arcades all the way to the Arno River. At this time of day, in the columns' shadows—diagonal black bars on pale yellow ground—one could often find crumpled Totocalcio lottery tickets.

English tourists in sleeveless T-shirts were taking pictures of each other on the Ponte di Mezzo, holding their arms flat against their sides and tilting like the Leaning Tower.

Clouds were drifting over the Corso Italia. Marco Ipranossian loitered a while in front of the department-store windows.

38

AT THE TRAIN station, an announcement came over the loudspeakers that the train to Florence had been delayed indefinitely. Marco Ipranossian waited fifteen minutes, then went to the station café to sit on a stool at the counter. From here, he could watch the departures and arrivals on a little screen attached to the wall. He leafed through the TV section of a daily newspaper. He drank a martini. He drank a glass of tomato juice, sucking the last drops of juice from between the ice cubes with his straw. There was a saucer in front of him which the barman regularly refilled with olives. He speared them with a toothpick. After a while, he began to feel queasy. He went back out to the concourse. The train from La Spezia had just arrived, right on schedule. Among the disembarking passengers was Lea. She was on her way home after a long day at the studio. She noticed an unusually large number of people crowding the platform. A man in a tan trench coat rushing past in the opposite direction paused just long enough to tell her that the service on several lines had been disrupted. Lea asked at a ticket booth whether the strike would be continuing all week. Her knit bag was bulging with tools. Bits of gravel stuck between the treads of her shoes were leaving faint scratches on the polished floor tiles.

The young woman at the booth—short blond hair, mustard-yellow blouse—asked for Lea's destination.

"Carrara."

Marco Ipranossian was standing just behind her. Lea could tell he was listening in on the conversation.

"You, too?" she said.

"No."

Lea asked him where he was headed.

"Pontedera."

"Where Piaggio is?"

"That's right. Vespa heaven."

Lea smiled. Marco Ipranossian had immediately noticed the dusting of white powder on her shirtsleeve, her disheveled hair, and the pair of plastic safety goggles peeking out of her bag.

While the woman in the booth was consulting her coworkers for information, Lea told Marco Ipranossian how the two days a week at Carrara recharged her energy so she could get through another week of school and family.

Marco Ipranossian looked at Lea and thought about this. Then he said he understood. He rummaged in the inside pocket of his jacket. He pulled out his wallet. He opened it and took from it a yellowed photograph, which he held out so she could see. It showed a man of about thirty with very dark, slicked-back hair. He was dressed in a collared shirt, a suit vest, pleated trousers that tapered at the ankle, and lace-up work boots. Behind him was a very tall building with vertical wood-plank siding. In the background—but here the photo was blurrier—two men in helmets could just be made out. They had their backs to the camera, facing instead toward the mouth of a tunnel and an object barely identifiable as a mine cart.

Marco Ipranossian said his father was an engineer and had managed copper mines in Alaverdi, one hundred and fifty kilometers north of Yerevan, in Armenia. He used to bring him rocks with iridescent blue flakes embedded inside. Marco Ipranossian didn't have time to finish his sentence. The young woman in the booth was tapping the knuckle of her index finger against the plexiglass window, near the Hygiaphone speaking hole.

"Miss . . . your information . . ." (Lea wasn't listening. The young woman spoke louder.) "Miss!"

Lea and Marco Ipranossian turned toward her, apologetic.

"The strike is today only," she said. "And sir, your train is arriving on platform three."

Lea and Marco Ipranossian thanked her. They walked a short distance together, then stopped in the middle of the concourse. They were surprised at themselves for having opened up to each other the way they did, and felt almost sheepish. They parted awkwardly, without saying goodbye. Two regretful glances. Then they walked off in opposite directions.

Outside, there was a sudden cloudburst. Rain could be heard lashing the pavement.

39

THAT NIGHT AT dinner, Marian asked Lea how her sculpture was coming. She had been working on it for more than three months.

Lea drew a sort of tuning-fork shape in the air with her finger. She closed off the top with a curved line. The sculpture was exactly like that, she said. With a hole in the middle.

This sounded rather abstract to Marian and Andrea. They didn't dare say anything, though. They didn't want to offend their daughter.

Lea told them what had happened to her a few hours earlier at the train station. She said she had talked to a man who must have been about forty. Tall. Thin. Black hair. Very dark green eyes. He was an Armenian who lived in a little village north of Pontedera.

Marian, who had just taken a sip of wine, nearly choked.

Lea said, "Do you want some water?"

Marian nodded. Lea handed her a glass. She drank a

few mouthfuls. She coughed a few times, tried to steady her breathing. Andrea asked if she was okay. Marian didn't answer. Instead, she got up and went to a console in the living room. She returned with a copy of *Il Tirreno* and spread it out on the dining room table. She put her finger on an article accompanied by two photographs: a scowling prefect exiting the courthouse, and a close-up of Marco Ipranossian, looking haggard. It was the same photograph the paper had printed four years earlier. The story took up only one column. It summarized the attempt on the prefect's life in a villa on the island of Elba. It reported the release of the man accused and said the investigation would continue. There was no commentary.

Lea read the article attentively and looked at the photographs. She was puzzled for a moment. Then she realized that the man she had met at the station was Marco Ipranossian.

One evening, Marian had told her about a difficult case she was working on. The nagging doubts that surrounded it. But she hadn't gone into detail.

Marian was also staring at the paper. She had remained standing. With her thumb, she twisted a ring around the little finger of her right hand: her mother's aquamarine.

She had accidentally put it in a glasses case which had lain buried under some papers on her desk for almost six months. That very morning, a deliveryman had brought her a big bouquet of white roses with a card. She had signed the receipt. Then she needed to clear room for the flowers on her desk. As she picked up a binder, she uncovered the case. She opened it. And she found her ring.

40

LEA WAS WATCHING a blackbird that had landed on her windowsill. She had left Italy in 2008. For the past year and a half, she had been studying at the University of California, San Francisco. She was doing a double major in geology and museology. She still took art classes regularly. Once a month, she traveled to northeast Los Angeles. She stayed there for a week at a time, in a disused elementary school at the foot of the San Bernadino Mountains, where a stonemason had set up an open-air studio.

Lea had taken a series of odd jobs in San Francisco. She had worked in the laundry room of a gym. As a trolley-car tour guide for Italian visitors. As a pet-sitter for families in the Marina District.

She lived at 2801 24th Street, in a Hispanic neighborhood, on the second floor of a house she shared with two other female students. The apartment was big and sunny, and included a deck, but the plumbing was a disaster. Every time someone took a bath or ran the dishwasher, water ran down the staircase.

Lea had made friends with some neo-grunge girls and some boys who wore nail polish. They would go to the movies together or have improvised picnics on the beach.

Every Sunday, Lea went to Oakland to visit her grandmother, who was still living in the same two-room apartment with the same chowder-gray wallpaper with thin red stripes.

*

Lea never could work out how the Carrara *operai* had folded newspapers to make hats.

41

ONE SATURDAY AFTERNOON, Lea took a group of Italian high-school students to see the de Young Museum. A newlywed Asian couple was posing for photographs just outside the entrance. They were walking very slowly in front the dimpled copper facade and the big picture window. In the smoked glass, behind the reflections of palm trees, the ghostly shapes of cafeteria furniture were just barely visible.

The bridegroom wore a black suit and shirt with a white tie. His face was partially hidden by the thick frames of his glasses. The bride was somewhat hampered by the frills and flounces of her white muslin dress. Her hair was gathered into a chignon, worn low on the nape of her neck. There was a pearl in the lobe of her visible ear. Her heels made a sharp, crisp sound on the flagstones.

The photographer directed the couple's gaze with his hand, pulling on an invisible string with his thumb and index finger.

An egg-shaped boom box had been set on the grass, off to one side, where it would be out of the frame. It was playing easy-listening pop music with piano and strings.

*

Lea led the teenagers through the museum. Contemporary blown glass. Art deco furniture made of wood and steel tubing. A nineteenth-century painting of migrant workers seated around a farmhouse table. A northern California landscape with violet trees and saffron-yellow hills.

Outside in the sculpture garden, Lea stopped the group for a long look at Barbara Hepworth's *Pierced Monolith with Color* in Roman stone.

42

WHEN THE GROUP had gone, Lea sat in Golden Gate Park, leaning her back against a tree trunk. She was worn out. She dozed. A man and a child who might have been twelve walked by, talking. Lea heard but didn't see them. The man was faltering over the name of a flower.

Late in the afternoon, Lea made her way over to La Oaxaqueña, a Mexican restaurant where two of her friends from art class, Martha and Lewis, were waiting for her. The streets were almost empty. It was this time of day that the fog usually rolled in off the bay. There was also a baseball game going on. The restaurant was tiny and didn't have a television. There was barely enough room to pull out the chairs from the tables. It was a perfect spot for conversation.

Lea, Martha, and Lewis had fish tacos garnished with diced onions and mint. The plates were edged with radish roses. As Lea was asking about the vanilla pastries on the dessert menu, a boy burst in, very excited. He announced—almost crowed—that the Giants had just beaten the Rangers. The whole neighborhood was out celebrating. There were shouts and whoops. A symphony of car horns. Firecrackers. Bottle rockets. Bouncing low-riders on Mission Street. Lea had never seen anything like it. Children ran around blowing shrill, high-pitched whistles at the top of their lungs, making the people nearby feel like their ears had popped.

*

As she was opening her bedroom window the next morning around dawn, Lea discovered a message written for her on the sidewalk, left by her friends Kai and Julie. Two sentences were visible:

come with us to the beach

And just below that:

hey dreamy
we missed you

Lea hadn't noticed them when she had come home the night before.

The sun was rising. Pink and orange clouds filled the sky.

A bird somewhere chirped its three-note song. The streets all around were hushed.

*

Later that morning, Lea called Kai and Julie. She asked them if they wanted to take the bus with her tomorrow to the San Rafael Rock Quarry.

After graduating from Paris's Ecole Normale Supérieure, CÉLIA HOUDART spent several years in the world of avant-garde theater before dedicating herself to fiction. Quarry is her third novel.

K. E. GORMLEY is a librarian and translator originally from Baltimore, now living in the Philadelphia suburbs.